The Midnight Masquerade

Behind every mask is a secret. And some secrets don't want to stay hidden

Rowan Hale

Contents

Prologue: An Invitation Cloaked in Shadows   1
1. The Masquerade Begins   5
2. First Dance with Darkness   9
3. Secrets Beneath Masks   13
4. Echoes of Fear   18
5. The First Sacrifice   23
6. A Dance Macabre   29
7. Shadows of the Past   33
8. Truth Behind the Mask   38
9. Midnight Revelation   42
10. Masquerade of Nightmares   46
11. The Final Hour   51
12. Unmasking Evil   55

Epilogue: Whispers at Dawn   59

Bonus Appendix: The Codex of Shadows - Recovered Fragments from the Black Veil Manor   63
Bonus Chapter: Behind the Scenes   67
Thematic Discussion Questions   71

Prologue: An Invitation Cloaked in Shadows

Under the cold, watchful eyes of the October moon, shadows danced silently upon empty streets, weaving through alleyways and whispering among leafless trees. Night held the village in its cold, velvet embrace, stilling even the bravest hearts.

Yet amid this unsettling tranquility, a solitary figure moved with sinister grace. Cloaked in heavy robes darker than midnight itself, the figure slipped through the sleeping village like a whisper of smoke. A deep hood hid its features, casting an impenetrable darkness over a face no living eyes had clearly seen. Only two piercing eyes, cold as winter stars, occasionally caught the pale light, flickering with an eerie, timeless intelligence.

Within gloved fingers rested a small satchel, embroidered meticulously in silver thread—an intricate pattern of vines intertwining with symbols from a forgotten tongue. The figure approached houses and shops alike, pausing thoughtfully before certain doors. It knew intimately the burden each occupant carried—every dark dream, every secret ache hidden behind carefully maintained masks.

At the doorstep of an ivy-covered cottage, the figure paused.

Beyond the door slept a woman tormented nightly by envy, whose desire burned brighter than embers in a dying hearth. With deliberate care, it extracted an invitation from the satchel—heavy parchment edged in gold and sealed shut with rich crimson wax stamped by an emblem of an ornate mask. Silently, it slid beneath her doorway, a whisper of promise entering her home.

Then onward, past shuttered windows and dormant gardens, the messenger drifted towards the great house upon the hill. Here resided a wealthy merchant, consumed by greed, whose heart craved what no amount of gold could purchase. Another invitation, another silent gift of temptation, slipped delicately beneath his threshold.

From one shadow to another, beneath balconies and through twisted gates, the messenger continued its silent work, bestowing these cursed invitations upon those whose secrets throbbed with desperation—souls willing to surrender anything, even innocence, for the fulfillment of their hidden, haunting desires.

When at last the satchel lay empty, the messenger stepped into the center of the quiet village square. Beneath the pale, merciless gaze of the October moon, it lifted its hood slightly. Moonlight brushed against an ageless face, pale as alabaster, framed by strands of raven-dark hair, eyes cold with unfathomable knowledge. Lips parted, forming words so faint they might have been mistaken for wind, yet sharp enough to pierce into the deepest, most hidden recesses of the recipients' minds:

"Come, reveal your truth... if you dare."

The whisper echoed through the sleeping village, seeping into dreams, turning them feverish and dark. Hearts quickened; sleeping eyes fluttered open with sudden terror, uncertain if they'd truly heard or merely imagined that chilling invitation.

With a final, satisfied glance, the messenger faded slowly into darkness, merging once more into shadows as if it had never truly existed. The village returned to silence, but an uneasy presence lingered—like the breath of something ancient and hungry, awakened from slumber, awaiting patiently for those brave or foolish enough to answer its call.

In mere days, beneath masks and cloaks, behind silks and satin finery, these chosen guests would come. Drawn irresistibly to a masquerade that promised everything they'd secretly longed for.

Unaware, of course, that the price might be far greater than any desire they hoped to fulfill.

The Masquerade Begins

Olivia Grey stood motionless before the looming iron gates of Ravenwood Manor, her breath forming delicate clouds beneath the moon's indifferent gaze. The manor towered like a phantom castle from nightmares long forgotten, its pointed spires piercing the velvet night. Ornate wrought-iron gates creaked open slowly, seemingly of their own accord, inviting yet menacing. Olivia tightened her grip on the forged invitation, feeling its parchment suddenly fragile in her trembling fingers.

"Midnight Masquerade," she whispered softly, voice tinged with determination and dread in equal measure. Her journalistic instincts had compelled her here, seeking answers to whispers of dark promises made beneath masks and shadows. Yet now, as she took her first hesitant step onto the estate's ancient grounds, Olivia could not help but feel the unsettling tug of a deeper mystery calling to her—one she feared might never release her once embraced.

The pathway to the manor was illuminated by lanterns suspended from gnarled, leafless trees, their flickering flames casting twisted shapes across the fog-shrouded path. Guests, silent as ghosts, drifted past Olivia in rich gowns and cloaks that shimmered like liquid shadows, their masks glittering cruelly beneath pale moonlight. Each concealed face seemed to harbor a secret, an unspeakable truth lurking just behind the ornate porcelain, silver filigree, and obsidian silk.

As she walked cautiously along the pathway, Olivia felt an uncanny awareness—an oppressive gaze from unseen eyes in the shadows. She glanced over her shoulder but saw only swirling mist and motionless statues, their frozen eyes seeming to follow her every move. She quickened her pace, pulse racing in sudden anxiety.

Crossing into the grand ballroom, Olivia drew a sharp breath at the lavishness that unfolded before her eyes. Opulence dripped from every corner—high vaulted ceilings adorned with gilded carvings, crystal chandeliers shimmering like captured stars, mirrors framing the room, multiplying its surreal splendor infinitely. Yet beneath this grandeur lay something subtly distorted and wrong, like the reflection of a beautiful face in shattered glass.

Guests filled the room, a mesmerizing sea of anonymous elegance. Laughter bubbled from painted lips, and secretive whispers lingered in the air, drifting in rhythm with the eerie, haunting strains of the masked orchestra's melody. Olivia forced herself forward, weaving into the tapestry of shadowy strangers, determined to uncover what lay hidden beneath this glittering façade.

As Olivia mingled, pretending to sip from a goblet she dare not actually taste, she overheard fragments of whispered conversations laced with anticipation and unease:

"*The Host chooses carefully,*" murmured a masked woman clad in crimson, voice hushed yet tinged with fearful longing.

The Midnight Masquerade

"*Fulfillment always comes at a price,*" replied her companion, his voice trembling slightly.

Olivia's stomach tightened. What was being promised here? She felt their anxiety mirrored in her own fluttering heart. Nearby, a guest in a raven-feathered mask briefly turned, and Olivia glimpsed eyes filled with a strange, almost inhuman hunger. A shiver traveled down her spine, cold and electric.

Stepping back from the crowd, Olivia paused near a mirrored wall, its glass slightly warped. As she stared into its depths, she saw her reflection subtly distort—a trick of light perhaps, but unsettling nonetheless. The eyes behind her own mask seemed to glitter briefly, as though alive independently, hungry for secrets hidden beneath her facade.

An icy chill rushed over her, heavy and oppressive, like a whisper of warning in her ear. Olivia turned sharply, expecting someone behind her, but saw only masked faces engaged in their silent charades. Her heartbeat quickened, instinct screaming a quiet alarm: she was being watched—not merely by curious guests, but by something older, colder, and infinitely more dangerous, concealed just beyond the edges of her perception.

Suddenly, the heavy chime of the gilded clock echoed through the ballroom, silencing all conversations at once. Olivia felt the vibration resonate through the polished marble beneath her feet, each toll striking her nerves like blows. Midnight had arrived, marking the true beginning of the masquerade.

Every masked face turned expectantly toward the grand staircase. Olivia followed their gazes, heart thundering, as a shadowed figure emerged with deliberate, regal grace. Tall, wrapped in velvety darkness, the Host descended slowly, each step calculated and confident. His mask gleamed, masterfully crafted, its visage both alluring and chillingly predatory.

A hushed breath of collective reverence and fear filled the ballroom, and Olivia's pulse quickened as his eyes scanned the crowd before suddenly fixing upon her own. The Host's gaze penetrated Olivia like a cold blade, stripping away her carefully crafted disguise, seeing into the core of her hidden motives.

Panic surged within her.

Did he already know why she had come? Had her secret been exposed even before her investigation truly began?

The Host offered a barely perceptible nod, his masked lips curving into a faint, unsettling smile—acknowledgment or warning, Olivia could not tell.

She could feel it now, a certainty rising within her bones: there was no turning back. The Midnight Masquerade had begun, and Olivia Grey, like every guest around her, was now trapped in a game whose rules were cloaked in shadow—and whose stakes might well be her very soul.

First Dance with Darkness

As the final, resonant chime of the clock echoed and faded into ghostly silence, every masked face turned upward, their attention collectively drawn to the shadowed balcony overlooking the ballroom. Olivia felt the atmosphere tighten as the guests held their breath in anticipation, her own pulse quickening beneath the glittering porcelain of her mask.

A figure emerged from the velvet darkness, stepping gracefully into the warm glow of the chandelier. Tall and commanding, he descended the grand staircase with an ethereal elegance, his footsteps soundless as if he floated rather than walked. Olivia found herself transfixed by his movements, precise and confident, yet utterly enigmatic. His attire was a study in midnight elegance—deep black velvet embroidered in patterns of ivy, glimmering faintly with silver threads that caught and reflected the wavering candlelight. Most striking was the mask covering his face—exquisite silver filigree intertwined with polished obsidian, sculpted into the haunting visage of a melancholy angel, beautiful yet infinitely sorrowful.

Whispers rippled through the gathered crowd, an awed hush tinged with barely suppressed excitement. Olivia felt the pull of the

Host's charismatic presence and quickly strengthened her resolve. She had not come here to be seduced by theatrics; she had come to expose whatever sinister reality lay hidden behind this opulent façade.

The Host reached the ballroom floor and raised a hand to silence the murmurs, his movements delicate, yet power radiated from every subtle gesture. When he finally spoke, his voice was like silk, smooth and enchanting, yet edged with a cool and tantalizing threat.

"*Friends,*" he began softly, his eyes gleaming behind the mask, piercing through each guest, "*you have come here tonight burdened by secrets, desires left unfulfilled, truths begging to be unleashed.*" He paused, allowing his words to sink deeply into the assembled guests. "*Before dawn touches this manor, you shall taste the sweetest nectar of your dreams realized—or face truths you have long tried to bury.*"

A tremor of excitement passed through the masked gathering, their whispered gasps betraying anticipation and dread intertwined. Olivia carefully studied their reactions—eager, fearful, but unmistakably captivated. Whatever dangerous game was afoot, she realized, the guests had willingly become players, lured by the Host's promise.

The masked orchestra resumed their haunting melody, strings weeping gently, as the guests moved toward each other, pairing off in a waltz dictated by music that seemed to weave a spell of its own. Olivia moved forward hesitantly, careful to remain inconspicuous amid the dancers. She blended into the dance, maintaining watchful distance, alert for any signs of danger.

Yet her curiosity drew her attention back toward the Host. He glided seamlessly through the swirling couples, an elegant predator moving effortlessly among prey, pausing occasionally to whisper into the ears of certain dancers. Olivia observed with growing unease that each whispered exchange left guests visibly shaken yet strangely euphoric, as if their hidden longings had just been glimpsed by this enigmatic figure. Some stumbled slightly, momentarily disoriented, eyes briefly clouded before clarity returned.

Olivia's unease blossomed into full suspicion—whatever power

The Midnight Masquerade

the Host wielded was not natural. He moved too swiftly, too silently, as though the manor itself allowed him passage, bending shadows to conceal him.

Suddenly feeling exposed, Olivia slipped from the dance floor and retreated into a shadowed alcove behind heavy velvet curtains. She exhaled quietly, grateful for the brief concealment, until a sudden chill crept along her spine—a sensation of icy breath whispering directly against her neck.

"*Miss Grey,*" a voice murmured softly, dangerously close. Olivia spun around, pulse pounding, to find the Host standing mere inches away, his presence commanding and suffocating at once. He had approached so silently she hadn't sensed him, and now she felt cornered, stripped of defenses.

"*Do I startle you?*" His voice was barely louder than a whisper, yet it resonated deeply within her bones. "How brave of you to enter my domain under false pretenses."

Olivia fought panic, forcing herself to remain composed. She tilted her chin defiantly, despite her heart hammering beneath her chest. "I don't know what you mean," she said carefully, striving for confidence she scarcely felt.

The Host leaned closer, the candlelight casting unsettling shadows beneath his elegant mask. "You hide your desires well—but beneath that mask, your truths scream louder than anyone's. You came seeking answers," he paused, "yet I wonder, Olivia, if you're prepared to pay the price once you have them?"

Before she could respond, he gently turned her toward the ballroom. With a graceful sweep of his hand, he directed her gaze to a large, ornate mirror on the opposite wall. Her reflection stared back —then rippled and distorted, momentarily shifting into something else entirely. Olivia recoiled in horror as her image warped, becoming a twisted reflection, eyes sunken and shadowed, mouth agape in silent torment, her deepest fears and insecurities vividly exposed.

Gasping, Olivia snapped her eyes back to confront him, but

found only empty darkness behind her. The Host had vanished, leaving her alone and trembling.

Slowly regaining composure, Olivia moved carefully back toward the ballroom. Her mind raced, the Host's words still echoing in her ears, his veiled threat haunting her. The masquerade's opulence seemed brittle now, beauty masking decay. Olivia overheard anxious murmurs among guests; many recounted seeing visions—twisted reflections of themselves in mirrors and polished surfaces. Each vision seemed uniquely horrifying, tailored specifically to their hidden fears.

Olivia felt reality unraveling subtly around her, glamour dissolving into dread. Beneath this grand charade, something darker stirred. The guests, blinded by their desires, were oblivious to the creeping madness—a madness carefully orchestrated by their charming, sinister Host.

With her pulse still unsteady, Olivia glanced around and caught sight of the Host slipping quietly through a hidden door concealed by rich drapery. Determination swelled within her chest. She knew now she was locked into something far more dangerous than she had anticipated—but retreat was impossible. She would follow, even knowing it would lead deeper into the shadows.

Taking a deep breath, Olivia slipped from the ballroom, silently approaching the hidden doorway. She hesitated only briefly, aware she was leaving behind the illusion of safety and descending into the unknown. Yet even as her fingers grasped the cold brass handle, she could not shake a dark certainty—this first dance with darkness would not be her last.

Secrets Beneath Masks

Olivia's fingers trembled slightly as she gently closed the hidden door behind her, sealing herself within a narrow, shadow-choked corridor. The cool air felt stale, heavy with centuries of silence. The candlelight flickered feebly against the rough-hewn stone walls, which bore strange markings carved deeply into the surface—glyphs that twisted and shimmered at the corner of her vision. She traced one gently, feeling a cold jolt pass through her fingertips, as though the walls themselves recoiled at her touch.

As she advanced cautiously down the cramped passageway, Olivia's sense of direction faltered. What she had assumed was a straight path twisted subtly, veering into unknown directions. She glanced back, panic prickling her spine—the door she'd entered through was gone, replaced by solid stone.

The realization settled deep inside her chest: the manor itself was shifting, changing, guiding her deeper into its dark heart.

After what felt like an eternity, Olivia emerged onto a secluded balcony overlooking an extravagant, circular chamber, gilded mirrors lining its curved walls. She instinctively shrank back into shadow, heart thudding painfully in her chest. This was no ordinary room—she felt the weight of countless secrets trapped within its ornate glass, whispering softly in unison like a chorus of invisible voices.

Below, elegantly masked guests stood in small clusters, their heads tilted closely as if sharing intimate confidences. Olivia strained her ears, and as though amplified by the peculiar acoustics, their whispers rose clearly, echoing vividly around her.

A woman wearing a sapphire mask feathered in glittering blue spoke urgently, her voice rich with malicious glee. "She trusted me completely," she confessed, tone edged with dark satisfaction, "but I needed her life to become mine. How could I resist taking it?" Her laughter, musical and cruel, sent icy ripples down Olivia's spine.

Across the room, a man draped in crimson velvet murmured feverishly, fingers twisting nervously. "They believe I'm their loyal partner," he hissed softly, lips twitching beneath his mask, "but when the sun rises, I'll have taken everything they treasure most." His voice trailed into a chilling chuckle, madness dancing in his eyes.

Olivia's stomach knotted painfully. Every confession was more shocking than the last, yet the guests appeared oblivious—or worse, indifferent—to the monstrous truths emerging from their lips.

A movement in the mirrored wall drew Olivia's gaze. Her breath caught sharply: the reflections were no longer mere images. They moved subtly, independently—faces in the glass twisted grotesquely, features elongating, morphing into monstrous visages that reflected the speakers' inner corruption. A noblewoman's graceful reflection stretched into a grotesque creature, mouth agape in silent agony, eyes wide and hungry. Another guest's reflection fractured into shadowy fragments, swirling like ink in water.

The guests seemed entranced, staring blissfully into their twisted reflections as though finally recognizing their true selves. Olivia covered her mouth, horrified and entranced simultaneously, understanding with chilling clarity: the mirrors fed upon these revelations, growing brighter, more alive with each sordid truth revealed.

Feeling sickened, Olivia stumbled back from the balcony, desperate to escape the oppressive revelations. But the corridors awaiting her were unfamiliar, twisted into a maddening maze. Doorways rearranged silently, hallways doubled back, looping endlessly.

Her heart pounded as she pressed her palms against a corridor wall, gasping sharply as it shifted slightly beneath her touch—breathing, alive, aware. A quiet, mocking laughter echoed faintly, reverberating within the stones, and she knew the mansion itself was toying with her, savoring her mounting fear.

A sudden noise made Olivia spin around sharply. From a shadowed archway emerged a man, tall and disoriented, his dark suit disheveled, silver half-mask askew. His deep blue eyes widened in surprise at seeing her.

"Who are you?" Olivia demanded, voice barely steady.

"Julian," he answered softly, glancing nervously down the corridor behind him. "I...I can't find my way out. This place—it's alive."

She relaxed only slightly, sensing genuine fear mirrored in his expression. Julian stepped closer, voice lowering to a hushed whisper. "I was invited here, promised something I've desired desperately," he confessed reluctantly. "But the mirrors, the walls...they're taking our secrets. They're using our fears against us."

Olivia felt a flicker of connection, fragile yet crucial. "Then we're trapped together," she admitted quietly. Julian nodded grimly, understanding passing silently between them.

. . .

Together they moved cautiously through winding corridors, but every turn heightened their fear—the mansion actively resisted their escape. Doors slammed suddenly; candles extinguished one by one, leaving only oppressive darkness and whispered laughter. Olivia shivered, feeling unseen eyes tracking them relentlessly, always just beyond sight.

She clutched Julian's arm instinctively as another mocking laugh reverberated through the walls, closer, clearer, echoing with cruel amusement. "It's him," Julian breathed shakily, voice heavy with dread. "The Host."

Finally, desperate for refuge, they stumbled into a dimly lit study—an ancient, dust-covered room lined with shelves of weathered books. Julian moved quickly, pulling down a thick diary, pages yellowed and brittle.

Olivia leaned over his shoulder as he flipped frantically through it, breath catching sharply at handwritten entries detailing past masquerades. Each ended tragically: guests vanishing, madness consuming survivors, their fates sealed by the mirrors and their own hidden truths.

The final, frantic entry was written in shaking script, ink smudged by tears long dried:

"Beware the mirrors, for they reveal not lies—but truths far worse than death."

As the words settled heavily between them, chilling laughter echoed clearly through the room, rich and dark, unmistakably belonging to the Host himself.

Fear surged wildly in Olivia's chest, realization dawning that escape was impossible—the manor had claimed them. As if to punctuate her dread, a distant scream pierced the silence—raw and full of agony, abruptly silenced.

The Midnight Masquerade

Julian turned pale, gripping her hand tightly. "We can't let it break us," he whispered fiercely, desperation edging his voice. "Whatever secrets you have, guard them. This house thrives on confession."

Olivia nodded, steeling herself against the rising tide of panic. But deep down, she knew it might already be too late. The masquerade had become a trap, carefully baited with desires, guilt, and fear—an elegant snare crafted by a place that feasted greedily upon secrets, pain, and dark revelations.

And as Olivia stood frozen beside Julian, trapped within corridors that breathed and mirrors that mocked, she realized the terrifying truth: they were now part of the mansion itself, forever ensnared beneath masks of their own making.

Echoes of Fear

Olivia stood silently beside Julian in the dim, oppressive study, their breathing shallow, mingling nervously in the candlelit gloom. She watched as shadows trembled on Julian's pale features, reflecting his inner turmoil. The mansion felt as though it watched them, unseen eyes probing their every hesitation.

Julian's fingers trembled as he pushed a hand through his tousled dark hair, finally breaking their tense silence. "I shouldn't have come here," he whispered, voice quivering with regret. His eyes, haunted and tired, avoided hers. "I should've known the promises were too good to be true."

Olivia stepped closer, sensing his vulnerability. "Promises? Julian, what exactly brought you here?"

He swallowed hard, gaze still fixed on the floor. "Music. Fame. All I ever wanted was recognition, respect for my art. But I lost my inspiration, my ability—I was nothing. Then someone offered a way to reclaim it. Someone... something sinister."

His voice trailed off into silence, and Olivia's heart tightened. Julian's pain was palpable, his secret heavy enough to crush him.

"Tell me," Olivia urged softly, placing a gentle hand on his arm. "You're not alone. Whatever it is, I need to understand."

Julian met her gaze finally, eyes wide with dread. "I think the one who offered me that deal is our Host."

Determination sharpened Olivia's features. "Then we have no choice but to keep moving forward."

Together, they exited the study into the shadowed corridor beyond. Doors lined the passageway, their wood blackened with age, etched with warnings in faded runes that seemed to writhe slightly as they passed. Olivia hesitated in front of a particularly ominous door, engraved with symbols she couldn't understand yet instinctively feared.

Julian tensed beside her. "Maybe we shouldn't—"

"We have to," Olivia said firmly, pushing the heavy door open, its ancient hinges screaming in protest. "The answers are here."

The door revealed a vast music room, ghostly in its abandonment. Dusty instruments filled the shadows—violins, harps, and a grand piano, their polished surfaces dulled by time. Olivia stepped cautiously inside, feeling immediately that something was deeply wrong here. The silence felt oppressive, as if a thousand unheard melodies were trapped within the walls.

Julian moved automatically toward the piano, his expression glazed, eyes distant. He touched its yellowed ivory keys gently, almost reverently. To Olivia's astonishment, Julian began to play, fingers gliding effortlessly across the keys. A haunting, sorrowful melody filled the air, so deeply melancholic it brought tears to her eyes.

"How do you know this song?" she asked breathlessly.

Julian's fingers stilled abruptly, voice shaking with dread. "Because I wrote it. Long ago, when darkness first swallowed me."

. . .

He turned to Olivia, anguish in every line of his face. "Years ago, I was desperate. My music was fading, my soul drying up. A man came to me—a shadow really, promising that my name would live forever, that my talent would become legendary. All I had to give in return was something he called trivial, something I hardly understood."

Olivia moved closer, heart pounding with dread. "What did you give?"

Julian closed his eyes, tears trembling on his lashes. "My soul. And now he's come to collect."

His words echoed into the emptiness of the room, a chill sweeping through Olivia as she grasped the terrible truth. Julian was no ordinary guest; he was trapped by a supernatural pact, enslaved by promises that had turned deadly.

Unable to linger, Olivia urged Julian forward, deeper into the mansion. Soon, they entered a hidden gallery filled with grotesque sculptures, paintings of twisted scenes of madness, and horrific statues carved from bone and wax. The figures appeared agonized, captured forever in silent screams.

"Dear God," Julian breathed in horror. "These aren't artworks... they're victims."

Olivia stepped closer, horrified to realize he was right. The sculptures moved ever so slightly, eyes flickering with trapped awareness, eternally reliving their torment.

"They're trophies," she whispered, voice shaking. "All who came before us."

Near the gallery's far wall, Olivia discovered an old, partially burned portrait depicting the Host. Dated centuries ago, the figure's haunting elegance matched their enigmatic captor perfectly. Scattered notes lay at her feet, written frantically in faded ink:

"He never dies. He feeds on secrets and despair. Escape is impossi-

ble. Beware the heart of the manor—it binds him, sustains him forever."

Her voice cracked as she read aloud, dread filling her bones. Julian reached out, gripping her hand desperately, eyes wide with horror.

"We must find that heart," he said shakily. "It's our only chance."

Escaping the gallery's suffocating dread, Olivia and Julian stumbled blindly into yet another hidden chamber. Immediately, their blood turned to ice. The room was filled floor-to-ceiling with porcelain dolls, hundreds of tiny, glass eyes glittering coldly, lifeless smiles painted cruelly upon delicate faces.

Then came the whispers—first soft, then deafening, a cacophony of voices echoing their deepest fears, secrets, regrets:

"Failure. Fraud. Your soul belongs to darkness." Julian recoiled, covering his ears.

Olivia heard her own voice, sharp with accusation: *"You came here chasing glory. Your curiosity will cost your life."*

Madness clawed at the edges of her sanity, threatening to engulf them both.

Then laughter burst sharply through the whispers—the Host's voice, richly amused, dripping with mockery.

"Poor Julian," his voice purred through the dolls, sadistically tender. "Did you truly think fame was free? And Olivia, brave Olivia—how many secrets do you hide behind that mask?"

Rage surged within Olivia, defiant in the face of despair. "You're nothing but a coward hiding behind tricks!" she shouted furiously.

The dolls fell suddenly silent, leaving only the chilling echoes of her voice.

The Host's laugh returned, quieter but dangerously cold. "We'll see, Olivia."

. . .

The dolls now silent, Olivia and Julian clung together, both trembling violently. Julian's voice broke the silence, resolute despite the terror in his eyes.

"The heart of the manor—it has to exist. Destroying it could free us, maybe break this endless curse."

Olivia nodded, breathing deeply to steady herself. "Then we find it—no matter what horrors lie ahead."

As they left the chamber, the dolls' porcelain eyes followed silently, tiny heads turning slowly to watch their exit, sinister smiles widening impossibly in the shadows. The whispers returned, softer, conspiratorial—hinting darkly at horrors still hidden in the mansion's core.

Olivia felt the corridor shift subtly behind them, sealing their path backward forever. The mansion had closed around them like a predator's jaws.

With dread pulsing through every step, Olivia and Julian moved deeper into the darkness, bound together by fate, determination, and fear—unaware that the mansion's deadliest secrets were yet to come.

The First Sacrifice

The oppressive quiet of the corridor pressed down upon Olivia and Julian, thick as velvet darkness. They moved cautiously, each creaking floorboard beneath their feet amplifying their anxiety. Olivia's pulse hammered relentlessly in her ears, her senses heightened, alert to the smallest disturbance.

Suddenly, an ear-splitting scream tore violently through the silence—a desperate, agonized cry echoing through the manor, filled with such raw terror that it froze Olivia mid-step. Julian clutched her arm tightly, his knuckles turning white, eyes wide with horror.

"God, no," Julian gasped, his voice shaking. "It's started."

Before Olivia could respond, the scream ended abruptly, plunging the mansion back into a silence even more terrible than before—a silence now stained permanently by death.

Compelled by urgency, Olivia rushed toward the sound, Julian trailing closely behind. They rounded a corner to find a crowd of masked guests gathered, their elegant composure shattered by panic and disbelief. Through the shifting mass, Olivia glimpsed a scene that made her stomach twist violently.

On the polished marble floor lay the crumpled body of a woman dressed in an exquisite emerald silk gown, now horribly stained crimson. Her porcelain mask lay shattered nearby, revealing her face frozen in absolute terror, eyes wide and unseeing, mouth agape as if her final breath had been a scream.

Most disturbing was the cause of death: jagged shards of mirror glass protruded gruesomely from her throat and chest, shimmering grotesquely in candlelight, reflecting the horrified faces of onlookers back at them, twisted and distorted.

Julian turned away, gagging, as Olivia steadied herself, forcing down her panic to examine the scene carefully. Something about the mirrors felt profoundly sinister—they weren't merely broken; the glass seemed deliberately positioned, arranged almost artistically around the corpse.

A ripple of fear surged visibly through the guests. Whispers quickly rose to frantic murmurs, panic feeding on itself as guests backed away in fear and suspicion, their masks now emphasizing rather than hiding their dread.

"Who did this?" someone whispered harshly.

"It could be any of us," another replied shakily. "We're all trapped here."

Suspicion blossomed rapidly into paranoia, alliances fracturing instantly as the crowd fragmented, casting wary, accusing glances at one another. Olivia watched in mounting horror, recognizing this as part of the Host's cruel design—forcing guests to confront their worst fears by turning them violently against one another.

Julian, visibly distressed, gripped her arm. "We need to leave before this gets worse."

"No," Olivia whispered back firmly. "We need to understand. There's meaning in this. We can't run yet."

The Midnight Masquerade

. . .

As chaos simmered dangerously, a sudden, unnatural hush spread swiftly through the crowd. All heads turned in unison toward the far end of the room, where the Host had silently appeared, standing motionless, framed by flickering candlelight. His presence instantly commanded fearful attention.

Slowly, with chilling calmness, he moved toward the fallen guest, footsteps utterly soundless. The guests instinctively parted, creating a fearful semicircle around him. Olivia watched intently as the Host knelt beside the body, inspecting it with detached curiosity, his silver-and-obsidian mask betraying no emotion.

After a moment, he rose gracefully, his voice clear and resonant yet unnervingly serene. "My dear guests, fear not. Such tragedies, while regrettable, are merely the first notes in tonight's grand symphony." His masked face turned slowly, surveying their fear-stricken faces. "The game has just begun."

Olivia shivered violently at his cold confidence. The Host's composure suggested absolute control; this murder was no unexpected accident—it was carefully orchestrated.

As the Host turned, his eyes briefly met Olivia's gaze, holding hers in a silent, chilling challenge. Olivia stiffened, sensing he knew exactly what she suspected. Beneath his veneer of elegant control lay a monstrous purpose—his calmness wasn't merely confidence; it was dominance.

She glanced at the shattered mirrors again, her breath catching. The fragments, even broken, continued reflecting shadowed figures, faces trapped in expressions of agony. Olivia understood suddenly: the mirrors weren't simple decoration. They were supernatural conduits, instruments of entrapment or punishment—feeding off human fear and despair.

Julian followed her gaze, whispering fearfully, "The mirrors. They're consuming her."

As servants arrived at the Host's quiet gesture, silently beginning to remove the body, Olivia discreetly stepped closer to examine the mirrors more closely. Fragments gleamed maliciously, reflections shifting unnaturally. Faces appeared within the glass—ghostly, tormented figures pressing desperately from inside.

Julian pulled her back urgently. "They're trapped souls, Olivia. Every broken mirror holds someone he's claimed."

Olivia's throat tightened painfully. "Then death here isn't the end—it's a beginning of eternal torment."

Back in the grand ballroom, panic swiftly morphed into paranoia. Guests whispered accusingly, forming wary factions. The once unified gathering now splintered dangerously, masks failing to hide desperate fear and suspicion.

"I saw you with her earlier!" a woman accused hysterically.

"You wanted her dead—you envied her!" another shouted bitterly.

Olivia watched with growing dread as rationality dissolved into madness, the elegant masquerade devolving rapidly into a sinister game of survival and accusation.

Julian trembled visibly beside her, voice raw with anxiety. "They're losing their minds. We'll be next if we stay."

"No," Olivia insisted quietly. "We must remain. We need to stop him before this madness takes us all."

But Julian's composure fractured further, his sanity fraying visibly. He paced nervously, muttering darkly, eyes darting fearfully around the room.

"I made a deal," he confessed quietly, voice ragged with fear. "What if I'm next? He knows I betrayed him."

Olivia steadied him, forcing calm into her voice. "We won't let that happen."

Yet privately, she worried deeply. Julian's stability seemed dangerously fragile. Whatever hidden darkness haunted him could soon unravel completely, endangering them both.

As the guests dispersed fearfully into smaller groups, the Host approached Olivia smoothly, his presence radiating subtle menace. His voice lowered intimately, dripping with warning.

"You are brave, Miss Grey—but foolish. Your friend harbors secrets darker than you imagine. Secrets that will doom you both."

Defiant, Olivia met his gaze fiercely. "You're responsible for her death."

The Host leaned closer, his voice a sinister whisper. "Death is merely the mirror's reflection of one's darkest truth. Be careful what truths you seek."

Before Olivia could respond, he vanished into the shadows, leaving her shaken yet determined to defy him.

Throughout the manor, fear intensified. Guests withdrew into paranoia and suspicion, isolating themselves behind locked doors, barricaded rooms, or mistrustful groups.

Julian clung desperately to Olivia, panic poisoning his mind. "We're running out of time. I feel it—I'm slipping away."

Olivia forced composure she didn't feel. "Stay with me. We must find the heart of the manor—destroying it might free everyone."

Yet uncertainty clawed silently within her, echoing Julian's despair: escape might already be impossible.

. . .

As Olivia and Julian stepped deeper into shadowed corridors, the mansion subtly rearranged itself around them. Doors vanished behind, halls twisted unpredictably, sealing escape routes completely.

The manor's grip tightened ominously, ensuring guests had no choice but to continue this grim masquerade of death and revelation. Olivia felt the manor's hunger intensify—she sensed it eagerly awaiting another sacrifice, another tragic echo reverberating through its halls.

And as darkness enfolded her further, Olivia realized bitterly the Host was right:

This gruesome murder was merely the first. The nightmare was only beginning.

A Dance Macabre

Panic surged through the mansion like a wildfire, obliterating the last traces of elegant restraint. Masked nobles screamed and pushed past one another, desperately clawing at doors and windows now sealed impossibly tight by unseen hands. Olivia watched, breathless, as the mansion itself appeared to savor their terror, rearranging its corridors subtly, reshaping passages into dead ends, trapping guests deeper within its sinister grasp.

Julian's fingers tightened painfully around Olivia's arm. His voice trembled, edged with dread. "The manor is alive. It won't let us leave—it wants us trapped."

Olivia moved swiftly toward a corridor she hoped might lead to safety, but even as they fled, she saw hallways shifting, doors vanishing into solid walls, sealing them deeper into the heart of the horror. They passed frantic guests who pounded helplessly against immovable doors, their cries echoing pitifully through halls marked by dark, hastily scrawled warnings:

"Only blood reveals the truth."
"Beware the mirrors—they hunger."

With each chilling message, Julian's breathing grew shallower, more panicked, as if the warnings spoke directly to him. Olivia's fear hardened into grim realization. "The Host is sacrificing us," she whispered, voice shaking but resolute. "Each death strengthens the ritual. We must stop him."

In a narrow hallway, they came upon a small group of frightened guests who had clustered together, their eyes wide with suspicion. Lady Evelyn clutched the tattered silk of her gown nervously, while Marcus, his once-confident presence now twisted by paranoia, glared at Julian.

"Safety in numbers," Marcus growled, suspicion darkening his voice. "But I don't trust him." He jabbed a finger toward Julian, who bristled immediately.

"I'm just as trapped as you are!" Julian snapped back, visibly distressed.

Olivia raised her hands quickly, trying to soothe frayed nerves. "We don't have time for accusations—we need to stay united if we're going to survive."

But even as she spoke, the air thickened with distrust, each wary glance and whispered accusation poisoning their fragile alliance.

Driven by desperation, Olivia led the tense group deeper into the mansion, discovering a hidden doorway behind ragged velvet curtains. Julian hesitated, sensing danger, but Olivia pressed forward determinedly. The group followed her reluctantly down ancient stone steps into a hidden chamber—a forgotten chapel lit by hundreds of candles flickering brightly, impossibly bright.

At the chapel's center stood a grotesque altar, blackened with centuries-old bloodstains. Surrounding it were mirrors, arranged carefully to reflect endlessly their horrified faces, twisted by candlelight into visages of despair. Marcus recoiled, disgusted. "This place is a temple to death."

Lady Evelyn moaned softly, hands pressed to her ears. "The mirrors...they whisper."

Olivia approached the altar slowly, heart hammering painfully.

"Every death is deliberate," she said, horrified by the truth. "We're trapped in a ritual, and our fear and pain feed its power."

Returning to the corridors above, their fragile alliance quickly unraveled. Marcus, paranoia seizing him completely, turned aggressively toward Julian. "You knew about this place! You're working with the Host!"

Julian's eyes flashed with desperation and anger. "I didn't know—I swear!"

Lady Evelyn shrank back fearfully, murmuring incoherently to herself. Olivia intervened swiftly, forcing a false calm into her voice. "Stop! This is exactly what the Host wants—us divided, helpless."

Privately, Olivia's trust in Julian was rapidly fading. She confronted him alone in the shadows, demanding honesty. Julian's eyes filled with haunted guilt. "I bargained for fame, Olivia. But the price was souls—I unknowingly drew others here. I can never forgive myself."

Olivia's heart twisted with conflicted sympathy and anger, yet she knew she needed him if they had any hope of escaping.

A sudden, agonized scream tore through the manor again, shattering their tense standoff. Racing toward the sound, they arrived at the grand staircase to find Marcus's lifeless body sprawled grotesquely, limbs twisted unnaturally. Blood pooled around him in elaborate, ritualistic symbols, mirrors arranged to capture his final moments of agony infinitely.

Julian recoiled, turning pale. Olivia choked down a wave of nausea, staring in horror. "Another sacrifice—he's feeding on their souls."

Above them, atop the staircase, the Host appeared silently, mask glinting cruelly in candlelight. The survivors fell into terrified silence, fixed in place by his chilling presence.

His voice resonated softly, tauntingly calm. "Each sacrifice brings us closer to the revelation. You are not mere victims—you are active participants. The dance has barely begun; fear is your truest partner now."

Guests scattered once again into desperate isolation, trust shattered beyond repair. Olivia turned fiercely toward Julian, determination hardening her resolve. "We must end this. Find the heart of this manor and destroy it—before anyone else dies."

Julian nodded shakily, his resolve sharpened by fear and desperation. "No matter what secrets remain between us, Olivia, I'm with you until the end."

Together, they pushed deeper into the mansion, feeling it tighten its grip around them. The walls seemed to breathe softly, mocking their efforts. Doors opened and closed spontaneously, directing them onward, deeper into darkness.

Julian whispered despairingly, "It's manipulating us, leading us exactly where it wants."

Olivia squared her shoulders, fighting the dread gnawing at her heart. "Then we'll face whatever awaits us head-on."

Just before entering another shadow-choked corridor, Olivia froze abruptly. Fresh blood glistened darkly on the wall, a chilling message dripping slowly:

"Truth revealed by blood alone—one more sacrifice remains."

Dread filled Olivia's chest, breath catching painfully in her throat. They understood clearly now—another would soon perish unless they intervened immediately. Olivia met Julian's fearful gaze, both knowing they were approaching their darkest moment yet, where survival might cost them everything.

Hand in hand, they stepped forward into the waiting shadows, hearts heavy with dread yet resolved to confront the horror at the heart of the manor's deadly masquerade.

Shadows of the Past

Olivia moved cautiously through corridors that twisted softly like living veins, the mansion pulsing around her, guiding her deeper into its malignant heart. Julian trailed closely behind, his breath ragged and uneven, eyes rimmed red with exhaustion and fear. Each step echoed dully, swallowed by shadows that seemed to whisper and laugh mockingly. Finally, after countless turns, they reached the towering doors of the manor's ancient library.

Pushing gently, Olivia felt the heavy doors reluctantly yield, revealing a room filled with towering shelves lost beneath centuries of dust. A ghostly silver moonlight filtered through stained-glass windows, casting distorted, unsettling shadows upon the faded spines of countless forgotten books. The air was thick, dense with decay and forgotten knowledge. Olivia's skin prickled uneasily, sensing eyes hidden behind shadows, watching intently.

Julian hesitated in the doorway, eyes wide, sensing danger. Olivia pressed forward, drawn instinctively toward a carved cabinet tucked away at the room's far end. Its ornate doors were etched with grotesque faces and symbols eerily reminiscent of the altar and mirrors they'd encountered before. She retrieved a rusted key she'd discovered earlier, fitting it carefully into the ancient lock. With a reluctant click, the cabinet opened, revealing a stack of worn leather journals bound tightly by strips of blackened cloth.

As Olivia lifted the first journal carefully, its fragile pages rustled quietly like dry leaves. Her breath quickened as she read the frantic handwriting of a guest who had attended a masquerade decades ago—his desperate narrative mirrored their current ordeal precisely. Lavish festivities, irresistible promises, and then the rapid descent into horror, paranoia, and death. Entry after entry spoke of mirrors that captured souls, of betrayals and sacrifices, until finally, the handwriting devolved into terrified scribbles, an incoherent plea for mercy left forever unanswered.

Julian, trembling, selected another journal, his voice faint and hollow as he read aloud, his words heavy with dread. "They promised me fame, music that could move the heavens...but the Host betrayed me. Now, my soul is bound to this place, eternally punished for my ambition."

His voice broke as he stopped, realization dawning horribly. Olivia saw the journal slip from his hands, falling open upon the stone floor. Julian sank heavily onto a dusty chair, head bowed in shame and despair.

"My God," he whispered hoarsely, "I'm not the first. I've condemned us all."

Olivia felt pity, yet mistrust lingered. Julian's guilt was genuine, but his past remained darkly entangled with the Host. "We must understand more," she insisted gently yet firmly, reaching for another journal.

This one, older and stained with age, revealed a different tale: the manor's origins and the first masquerade. A nobleman, charismatic and power-hungry, had become obsessed with immortality. His handwriting began clear and rational but swiftly descended into frantic madness. Through forbidden magic, he bound his own soul irreversibly to the mansion, cursing it eternally. Every Halloween, he hosted masquerades disguised as exclusive events, each one a ritual that harvested souls to sustain his endless life. Olivia's throat tightened painfully—the Host wasn't merely cruel; he was trapped in his own monstrous cycle, forever enslaved to the manor's hunger.

Julian paced nervously, eyes haunted, voice shaking. "He made a pact like mine. His soul forever chained to darkness. And I've been helping him without even knowing."

His distress deepened Olivia's internal conflict—she needed Julian, yet feared his vulnerability made him susceptible to the Host's manipulation. "We can still break it," she reassured, though doubt clung like frost to her words.

As Olivia continued flipping through the journals, her blood turned cold upon discovering detailed explanations of the mirrors' sinister purpose. They weren't just decorative—they were prisons, supernatural vessels holding souls eternally captive, their torment fueling the Host's dark immortality. Julian's hands shook visibly, recalling his own distorted reflections. "He's already taking me," he whispered fearfully. "I can feel pieces of myself slipping away."

The chilling revelation deepened Olivia's urgency—escape was not merely physical but spiritual. If they failed, their souls would join countless others in eternal torment.

Further into the cabinet, Olivia discovered letters penned by the Host himself, centuries old. His early words bore traces of genuine humanity—hopes, ambitions—but soon spiralled downward into chilling madness, reflecting his twisted journey from man to monster. For a fleeting moment, Olivia felt reluctant sympathy—he was not born evil; he had willingly stepped into darkness, corrupted by his desperate fear of death.

Julian reacted bitterly to Olivia's brief sympathy, his voice sharp with anger. "Don't pity him. He chose his fate and damned the rest of us. He deserves no compassion."

But Olivia recognized the tragedy behind the cruelty, the human soul warped beyond redemption by dark ambition. Still, she steeled herself, determined not to let empathy weaken her resolve. To break the cycle, she would need to face the Host directly, without hesitation.

As Olivia pieced together the horrific truth, she realized their only hope lay in finding and destroying the manor's heart—an ancient chamber hidden deep beneath the mansion, fiercely guarded by the spirits of the Host's victims. Julian nodded grimly, agreeing with painful desperation. "Whatever it takes, Olivia. We must end this."

But as they prepared to leave, the air in the library suddenly thickened, becoming oppressively heavy. Shadows deepened around them, whispers intensifying into anguished cries. Horrified, they watched as ghostly apparitions materialized, spectral faces twisted with eternal torment, reaching out imploringly.

Julian stumbled backward, choking out terrified apologies. Olivia grabbed his hand, pulling him toward the door. "Run!" she shouted desperately as they fled, echoes of the past victims' tortured pleas chasing them into the corridors beyond.

As they paused, catching ragged breaths outside the library, Olivia noticed a final journal lying open upon a small table. Its pages appeared freshly inked, words gleaming darkly beneath moonlight:

"Tonight the ritual reaches completion. Only blood willingly given can sever the curse. Beware who you trust."

Her heart stopped, ice flooding her veins. Olivia's gaze rose slowly, meeting Julian's troubled eyes. A silent understanding passed between them—an invisible, dangerous boundary drawn clearly now, trust replaced by wary suspicion. Julian's expression hardened, unreadable, deepening Olivia's dread.

With determination hardening her heart, Olivia turned toward the shadow-choked corridor ahead. Julian fell into step beside her, their alliance precarious, fragile, overshadowed by haunting revelations and fearful uncertainty.

Together, bound by shared desperation yet separated by mistrust, they moved forward into the mansion's darkest depths, where blood and sacrifice awaited, fully aware the next steps might force unbearable choices—choices that neither might survive.

Truth Behind the Mask

Olivia felt urgency pulse within her veins, driving her toward a desperate decision. With the library's revelations still haunting her, she knew the time had come to confront the remaining guests directly. She and Julian quickly rounded up the scattered survivors, each guest eyeing the others warily, suspicion simmering dangerously beneath forced civility. Lady Evelyn, Samuel, and Catherine stood nervously, their elaborate masks now hiding less and less of their growing dread.

Julian stood off to the side, visibly troubled, his presence deepening the tension in the room. Olivia felt their fragile alliance fraying like a thread pulled taut, yet she pressed forward, knowing they had little choice but to face the truth directly.

Taking a calming breath, Olivia turned first to Lady Evelyn, whose elegant demeanor had crumbled to fearful fragility. Olivia's voice softened, but her words were unyielding. "Evelyn, we need to know the truth. What brought you here?"

Lady Evelyn's lips trembled, her gaze darting anxiously around the room before finally settling on the floor. "Envy," she whispered miserably. "I envied another woman—a rival. I sabotaged her life to make myself feel superior. But it only destroyed her...and myself."

Her tearful confession hung in the air heavily, drawing murmurs of discomfort from the others. Evelyn's emotional vulnerability made her dangerously susceptible, Olivia realized grimly, marking her clearly as an easy target for the Host's manipulations.

Samuel shifted uneasily, glancing nervously toward Julian before defensively snapping, "Why interrogate us, Olivia? Perhaps your companion, Julian, knows more than anyone."

Olivia held her ground, eyes piercing into Samuel's evasiveness. "Your deflections only make you more suspicious, Samuel. What secrets brought you here tonight?"

Under her relentless gaze, Samuel finally cracked, voice trembling with guilt and fear. "Greed," he admitted bitterly. "I betrayed my partners—lied, cheated, stole. Ruined lives for profit." His eyes darkened with shame, but his admission ignited hostility among the group. Evelyn recoiled visibly, and Catherine raised an eyebrow coldly, further fracturing their brittle unity.

Olivia turned sharply toward Catherine, whose calm indifference unnerved her deeply. Catherine met Olivia's gaze steadily, unflinching. "You waste your time, Olivia. I came out of boredom, curiosity. Life is terribly dull without a thrill. I knew precisely what the Host promised, and frankly, the suffering of others matters little to me."

Her detached cruelty left the others speechless, stunned into horrified silence. Olivia sensed a deep threat in Catherine's icy demeanor, realizing she was perhaps the most dangerous guest of all—emotionless, remorseless, and willing to embrace darkness willingly.

Throughout the confrontations, Julian grew increasingly agitated, his hands trembling slightly, eyes filled with haunted guilt. His erratic behavior intensified suspicion, and the guests openly eyed him with growing hostility. Olivia drew him aside briefly, gripping his arm firmly. "You must hold yourself together, Julian. They're turning against you."

He pulled away bitterly, despair darkening his features. "Maybe they should. I brought this upon us. My soul was corrupted by ambition—how can you trust me when I don't trust myself?"

Olivia swallowed hard, torn between sympathy and doubt. His pain was genuine, but his instability threatened to undermine everything she fought to achieve.

Tension soon erupted into outright accusation, Samuel openly confronting Julian, his voice harsh with paranoia. "You sold your soul—who says you haven't sold ours too?"

Julian snapped, lunging forward angrily. "I'm no traitor!" Olivia barely intervened in time, forcing herself between them, her voice sharp with authority. "Enough! This fighting is exactly what the Host wants."

But Catherine stepped forward, her calm voice cold and cutting. "And who put you in charge, Olivia? Your motives aren't exactly pure. Why exactly did you infiltrate this masquerade? Professional curiosity—or personal obsession?"

The question hung in the air, thick with suspicion. Olivia faltered briefly, feeling their trust slipping away. But instead of denial, she raised her chin defiantly, embracing the uncomfortable truth. "My sister disappeared after attending a masquerade years ago. I came for answers, yes—but also justice. Does that make me less trustworthy, Catherine, or simply more committed?"

The guests hesitated, uncertain. Catherine smirked knowingly, yet said nothing more, allowing doubt to fester.

Julian, caught in a spiral of paranoia and guilt, finally reached his breaking point. He spun wildly toward Samuel again, voice shaking with barely contained panic. "He's working with the Host! He'll betray us all!"

Chaos erupted again, voices overlapping in confusion, accusations flying wildly. Olivia stepped in forcefully once more, grabbing Julian firmly, forcing him to face her. "Julian, look at me! Stop! We can't do this. We must remain united or we're lost."

Julian stared back blankly for a moment, then sagged heavily, defeated and emotionally drained. His voice cracked miserably. "He's already won. Don't you see? We've given him exactly what he wants."

As if summoned by Julian's despair, the Host's laughter filled the room, deep and mocking, emanating from everywhere at once. "Precisely, Julian. Such beautiful chaos you've all created. Fear and betrayal—your humanity makes you perfect pawns."

Guests recoiled fearfully, realizing their confrontation had precisely fulfilled the Host's twisted design. Olivia felt despair momentarily threaten her resolve. The Host's voice, rich with cruel amusement, addressed her directly. "Thank you, Olivia. You've exposed their weaknesses perfectly. Your actions ensure my victory."

Yet rather than crumble, Olivia drew strength from anger. She stood taller, defiance burning in her eyes. "You underestimate us," she retorted sharply into the empty air. "Your game ends tonight."

The Host's laughter faded slowly, echoing mockingly into silence, leaving them alone with their paranoia and fear.

Olivia turned resolutely toward the shaken guests, addressing them firmly. "We have only one chance left—to face the Host directly, to destroy the heart of this mansion. Distrust me if you must, but understand this clearly: unity is our only hope now."

Eyes met briefly, doubt and mistrust still lingering heavily, yet beneath suspicion lay a shared desperation for survival. Reluctantly, the guests nodded agreement, fragile alliances forming again from sheer necessity.

Julian met Olivia's gaze last, haunted yet determined. "I'll stand with you, Olivia. Whatever secrets remain, I'll face them beside you."

Together, bound by uncertainty yet driven by desperation, the fractured survivors stepped forward toward the mansion's heart, fully aware the truths waiting behind the Host's mask would demand sacrifice, pain, and possibly their very souls.

Midnight Revelation

Olivia's heartbeat echoed painfully in her ears as she led the fractured, frightened group toward the mansion's heart. Their fragile alliances, weakened by mistrust and fear, felt as thin as spider silk. Julian walked silently at her side, pale and withdrawn, his face drawn tight with anguish. Olivia felt a surge of anxiety, sensing that Julian bore a terrible secret he had yet to reveal.

At the threshold of a shadowed corridor, Julian stopped suddenly, touching Olivia's arm gently. His eyes, haunted and pleading, met hers. "We need to talk privately," he whispered, voice raw with desperation.

Nodding, Olivia followed Julian into a quiet alcove, distant enough from the others for privacy. Julian hesitated, gathering courage, before finally meeting her gaze. His voice shook as he spoke. "There's more you must know. My pact wasn't just my soul—I offered others as well, without truly understanding the cost."

Olivia's heart froze as Julian continued, tortured by shame. "The Host used me, Olivia. Through me, he drew countless souls to past masquerades—including your sister. Her fate is my fault."

Olivia felt as though the world had collapsed beneath her feet, betrayal and anguish roaring through her veins. Tears blurred her vision as fury battled grief within her. "Julian," she choked, voice trembling, "how could you?"

His head bowed miserably. "I was desperate, blinded by ambition. I didn't know then what the Host was doing—how he fed on their souls. When I finally understood, it was too late."

She felt torn, the urge to abandon him nearly overwhelming. Yet as Julian stood broken before her, Olivia glimpsed the genuine remorse etched deeply into his soul. Understanding slowly replaced her anger. Julian, too, was a pawn in the Host's merciless game.

"We can't change the past," she said finally, forcing strength into her voice. "But we can break this cycle now—together."

Julian nodded, eyes darkened by deep despair. "There's only one way. A willing sacrifice at the ritual's climax can break the curse. My soul, freely given, could weaken the Host's hold."

Olivia's chest tightened painfully, realization piercing her like a blade. "Sacrifice means death, Julian."

He met her gaze unflinchingly. "I know. But it's the only way to redeem myself—to save you and the others, perhaps even the souls I've condemned."

Swallowing her grief, Olivia understood Julian's resolve was absolute. She saw not only regret in his eyes, but a fierce determination born from the unbearable weight of guilt. Reluctantly, painfully, she accepted his choice. "I promise I won't waste your sacrifice. But if there's another way, I'll find it."

Returning to the anxious guests, Olivia and Julian soon encountered an ornate door carved deeply with ancient runes glowing faintly in the dim candlelight. Olivia recognized symbols identical to those found in the library journals and around the cursed altar. Julian studied them intently, murmuring fragments from memory, gradually deciphering their meaning.

"These runes bind the Host's soul eternally," Julian explained softly, fingers tracing the strange symbols. "He feeds on unwilling souls. But the curse can be undone—by a soul freely sacrificed at midnight, at the height of the ritual's power."

His voice faltered slightly. The group's fearful murmurs filled the tense silence that followed. Panic surged; voices rose angrily, accusingly, each survivor desperate to preserve their own life.

Catherine laughed bitterly, eyes cold. "And who among us is willing to die?"

Julian's expression hardened. Olivia saw his silent resolve, pain gripping her heart. He stepped forward firmly. "I will."

The room fell silent. Olivia stared at Julian, heart aching. "Julian, please—"

He shook his head gently, firm and determined. "This is my burden, my penance. It's the only way."

Olivia's throat tightened painfully, but she respected his courage. Her eyes shimmered with unshed tears as she nodded slowly. "Then I'll face the Host with you. Together, we'll weaken him enough to end this forever."

Despite lingering mistrust, the guests reluctantly agreed to assist, desperation overriding their fear. Julian drew Olivia aside one final time, his voice tender yet raw. "I never deserved your trust, Olivia, yet you gave it freely. Forgive me—for everything."

Tears finally slipped silently down her cheeks. "I forgive you, Julian. I just wish there was another way."

He touched her cheek gently, sadness shadowing his eyes. "If my sacrifice sets your sister's soul free, it's worth everything."

As midnight approached, the mansion reacted violently, desperate to stop their advance. Walls trembled, mirrors shattered explosively, shards spraying like silver knives. Ghostly apparitions appeared, souls trapped within the mansion pleading for salvation. Their anguished cries only strengthened Julian's resolve, reinforcing his courage to face the horror ahead.

Steeling themselves, Olivia, Julian, and the group pushed through resistance until reaching the ritual chamber hidden deep beneath the mansion. The vast chamber was filled entirely with mirrors, endlessly reflecting tortured, anguished faces—souls eternally trapped in torment.

At its heart stood the Host, calm, poised, eyes glittering darkly behind his silver mask. His presence radiated immense, ancient power. Olivia's breath caught sharply; Julian stood tall beside her, unyielding.

The Host's voice echoed softly, confidently. "So brave, yet so foolish. Do you truly believe sacrifice can undo centuries of power?"

Julian stepped forward defiantly, voice unwavering. "My soul is freely given. Your power relies on unwilling victims—but courage and sacrifice can break your curse forever."

The Host hesitated momentarily, a flicker of unease in his posture. Olivia sensed their advantage clearly now—Julian's courage had indeed shaken him.

Olivia lifted her chin, voice resonant with fierce determination. "Your power comes from fear and betrayal, but we stand united against you. Your curse ends tonight."

The Host laughed softly, arrogance masking the faint tremor beneath. "We shall see."

Midnight approached relentlessly. Julian turned toward Olivia one last time, their eyes locking in silent farewell. Olivia's heart tore painfully, yet she forced herself to remain strong, accepting his decision with aching pride.

Hand in hand, they faced the Host, prepared to confront darkness head-on, fully aware the price would be unbearably high—but willing to pay it, if it meant shattering the curse, saving innocent souls, and ending this eternal masquerade once and for all.

Masquerade of Nightmares

The stroke of midnight echoed like a funeral bell through the manor, shattering the fragile calm. Immediately, a surge of malevolent energy erupted violently, rippling outward from the ritual chamber. The mansion trembled as reality itself fractured, plunging every guest into personal nightmares crafted from their darkest fears.

Olivia stumbled, grasping Julian's hand tightly, her senses overwhelmed by the cacophony of screams reverberating down the corridors. Lady Evelyn's shrieks pierced the chaos first, high and tormented, filled with despair and guilt. Olivia turned, witnessing the once-elegant noblewoman clawing frantically at invisible assailants, eyes wide with madness as she pleaded with a rival only she could see, begging forgiveness that would never come.

Samuel collapsed nearby, sobbing uncontrollably as visions of those he betrayed crowded around him, their ghostly fingers reaching accusingly. "Please, forgive me," he wept, his voice a shattered whisper swallowed by the darkness. Catherine, who had previously been chillingly indifferent, finally broke under relentless apparitions mocking her callousness. She staggered backward, the glassy masks of those she'd harmed emerging from mirrors around her, their whispers relentless, stripping away her cold facade layer by layer.

Olivia's own breath froze in her throat as the manor turned its sadistic focus onto her. Her sister appeared before her, beautiful yet spectral, her eyes hollow with accusation and sorrow. "You left me here, Olivia," the apparition whispered, voice filled with betrayal. "You abandoned me. Now join me—there's no escape."

Tears blurred Olivia's vision, guilt threatening to consume her entirely. She felt Julian's grip tighten urgently, pulling her close. "It's not real," he shouted desperately. "Fight it, Olivia. They're illusions!"

With great effort, Olivia clung to Julian's voice, anchoring herself to reality. Around them, the mansion's power intensified, the air thick with dark magic exploiting every vulnerability. The Host's hunger fed greedily upon their collective madness, reveling in the fractured minds and shattered spirits of his victims.

Julian's eyes blazed with determination, even as his strength visibly faded. "We must confront him now," he gasped, urgency shaking his voice. "It's our only chance."

Olivia swallowed hard, her heart heavy, knowing Julian's decision to sacrifice himself was irreversible. Still, she drew strength from his courage, steeling herself against her grief. "Together, Julian," she promised fiercely. "He won't win."

They advanced toward the central chamber, fighting through visions that clawed at their minds. Each step felt impossibly heavy, reality distorting around them. Julian's face twisted in anguish as visions of those he'd unknowingly condemned emerged, their spectral forms pleading and cursing him in equal measure. Olivia gripped his hand tightly, anchoring him just as he had anchored her, until finally they reached the ritual chamber.

The Host stood at its center, a dark, imposing figure surrounded by mirrors pulsating with captured souls. He faced them calmly, coldly confident as he slowly removed his mask. Beneath it lay a visage of nightmares, flesh twisted grotesquely by centuries of dark magic and corruption, eyes burning with predatory hunger. Olivia recoiled instinctively, fear surging primal and raw within her, but Julian steadied her, his presence reassuringly defiant.

The Host's voice, now deep and distorted, resonated through the chamber. "Do you see now? This is true immortality, power born from human weakness and fear."

Without waiting, the Host unleashed his wrath, warping the chamber into a nightmarish realm of living shadows and shifting illusions. Reality fractured violently around them; Olivia and Julian were plunged into a relentless battle against illusions specifically crafted to exploit their emotional vulnerabilities. Horrifying images battered them: Olivia watched, heartbroken, as Julian appeared to betray her repeatedly, each vision crueler and more painful than the last.

Julian staggered, weakened by the relentless assault, yet somehow found strength to shout defiantly, "None of this is real! He's afraid of us—afraid of our courage!"

Olivia's mind cleared momentarily at Julian's words, and she seized the advantage. Stepping forward, her voice trembled with defiant anger. "You were human once! You traded humanity for this—an eternity of emptiness and suffering. You lost yourself to fear long ago."

For the first time, the Host hesitated, his monstrous form briefly flickering with uncertainty. Olivia pressed harder, confronting him with relentless emotional truth. "Your immortality is a prison, sustained by fear alone. Without it, you're nothing."

Julian, sensing the Host's weakening resolve, stepped forward decisively, his voice clear and unwavering. "My soul is freely given—to end your nightmare forever."

As Julian declared his sacrifice, a blinding surge of energy erupted from him, pure and radiant, starkly contrasting the darkness of the Host's corrupted soul. The Host roared furiously, desperation fueling his counterattack as he lashed out violently, the chamber shuddering under his rage. Julian staggered under the onslaught, pain etched deeply into his features, but he stood firm, courageously holding the ritual's destructive forces at bay.

The strength of Julian's willing sacrifice weakened the Host profoundly, breaking his concentration. Slowly, the illusions tormenting the other guests began to dissipate. Catherine, Samuel, and Lady Evelyn collapsed in exhaustion, sanity returning in fleeting, painful clarity. They gazed around, their faces hollow and broken by the psychological torment they had endured, recognizing their complicity and vulnerability, but also their narrow escape from eternal torment.

In a desperate final assault, the Host targeted Olivia directly, conjuring an illusion so powerful it nearly shattered her resolve—a perfect replica of her sister appeared once more, voice trembling with heartbreaking sincerity. "Please, Olivia," the apparition pleaded, tears falling silently. "End my suffering. Give yourself freely."

Olivia's heart shattered, grief threatening to overwhelm her completely. Yet as she wavered, Julian's voice reached her once more, gentle but firm. "It's another lie, Olivia. You're stronger than his illusions."

With painful determination, Olivia raised her head defiantly, refusing the Host's cruel manipulation. "I won't surrender to your lies. My sister deserves freedom, not eternal torment. You will never control me."

The Host shrieked in fury as Olivia's defiance further unraveled his remaining power, illusions collapsing completely. Severely weakened, he retreated into shadow momentarily, giving Olivia precious seconds. She rushed to Julian's side, gently holding him as his strength faded rapidly. Tears burned her eyes as she whispered fiercely, "Your courage gave us hope. I promise I'll finish this."

Julian's breathing became shallow, his eyes filled with peace despite the pain. "This was my redemption," he murmured softly. "End him, Olivia. Free us all."

Olivia stood, heartbroken yet resolute, fully aware the Host would soon strike again. The chamber trembled violently, the mansion's supernatural foundations fracturing irreparably. Steeling herself, Olivia knew the next confrontation would be her ultimate test.

Around her, the guests stirred weakly, watching with hollow eyes, barely holding onto sanity. Olivia met their gaze briefly, silently communicating her determination to finish what Julian's sacrifice had begun.

The shadows stirred violently as the Host, driven by primal desperation, prepared for his final, savage confrontation. Olivia squared her shoulders, drawing strength from Julian's sacrifice, prepared to confront evil head-on. Her voice rose strong and defiant, echoing through the collapsing chamber.

"It's time to end this masquerade."

The Final Hour

Julian stood resolute, a fragile figure illuminated by the shifting candlelight, yet embodying an extraordinary strength born from courage and regret. Olivia watched helplessly, her heart breaking as he stepped forward, facing the monstrous Host with unwavering determination. His voice trembled, but carried clear conviction.

"I give myself willingly," Julian proclaimed fiercely, his words echoing through the cavernous chamber. "My soul, offered freely, breaks your curse forever."

The instant those words left his lips, a blinding pulse of pure, radiant energy erupted from Julian, surging outward with violent force. Mirrors shattered instantly, the glass fracturing into countless shards that rained down like crystal tears, releasing anguished souls imprisoned for generations. Each freed soul passed through the chamber, their whispered gratitude caressing Julian softly before dissipating into the ether.

The Host screamed in primal fury, his monstrous form convulsing violently as Julian's sacrifice unraveled centuries of carefully woven enchantments. Reality itself trembled, foundations of dark magic collapsing rapidly around them. Olivia saw her moment, fleeting but undeniable, and moved instinctively forward.

Yet, even as she approached, grief and doubt surged painfully within her chest. The loss of Julian tore through her heart, threatening to paralyze her completely. Sensing her emotional turmoil, the Host rallied desperately, exploiting her grief and conjuring horrifying illusions designed specifically to destroy her resolve.

Suddenly, Olivia found herself standing alone, the chamber replaced by the painful familiarity of her childhood home. Her sister appeared before her, eyes pleading, sorrowful yet accusing. "You let me down," the vision whispered heartbreakingly, "you abandoned me, Olivia. It's your fault I'm gone."

Painful memories flooded Olivia's mind: her sister's laughter, warmth, and ultimately, her tragic disappearance that haunted Olivia relentlessly. Every regret, every lingering guilt resurfaced, threatening to drown her in despair.

But even within this torment, Julian's final act resonated deeply, a beacon cutting through her darkness. His courage, his redemption, sparked a fierce resolve within Olivia. Shaking her head defiantly, she faced the illusion head-on, her voice steady, tempered by pain yet unwavering.

"No," she declared firmly, meeting the vision's pleading gaze. "I made mistakes—but I refuse to let guilt control me anymore. You're not my sister. You're just another cruel illusion."

The vision faltered, distorted briefly, then dissolved into shadows. Olivia breathed heavily, empowered by her newfound emotional clarity. She understood now—accepting her fears and regrets weakened the Host's control, robbing him of the power derived from despair.

Yet the Host, despite being severely weakened, remained formidable. His monstrous form lunged violently from the darkness, tendrils of shadow and madness wrapping around Olivia, physically and psychologically suffocating her. Every muscle screamed in agony as he battered her mind relentlessly, flooding her thoughts with images of Julian's betrayal and her sister's death, desperately seeking to fracture her spirit.

Through the excruciating assault, Olivia focused fiercely on the truth of Julian's courage, rejecting the Host's manipulative lies. Each acceptance of her pain, each defiance of despair, weakened the Host further. His monstrous visage began flickering, stability unraveling rapidly.

Summoning her remaining strength, Olivia spoke firmly, her voice resolute and clear. "You preyed on human weakness and fear for centuries. But you're the weakest of us all—trapped eternally by your own cowardice."

The Host recoiled violently, visibly shaken. His power waned rapidly, Olivia's defiant courage dismantling his carefully constructed dominance.

Nearby, the surviving guests—Lady Evelyn, Samuel, and Catherine—slowly rose from the floor, their minds fractured yet awakening, inspired by Olivia's unwavering bravery. Their once-hollow eyes filled with tentative hope, silently urging her onward.

The mansion itself shook violently, walls cracking as supernatural bonds unraveled irreparably. In this chaos, Olivia suddenly saw a final, luminous vision—a gentle apparition of her sister, radiating warmth, sincerity, and love untouched by the Host's dark illusions.

"Olivia," the apparition whispered tenderly, eyes shining with forgiveness, "I never blamed you. Let go of your guilt. You've freed me, and so many others. Be strong now. Finish this."

Tears filled Olivia's eyes, her heart finally releasing years of pent-up grief. She nodded gently, peace washing over her as her sister's spirit faded, leaving behind only profound strength and clarity.

Desperate, the Host transformed once more, his monstrous form grotesquely shifting between human and nightmare. He pleaded with her now, voice trembling with genuine fear. "Mercy, Olivia—I can give you immortality, power beyond your dreams! Spare me!"

But Olivia shook her head, voice clear and unwavering. "You're beyond redemption. Your fear enslaved others, but now your fear has trapped you. This ends tonight."

The Host shrieked bitterly, desperation warping his monstrous visage further. Olivia took a deep breath, whispering a final farewell to Julian, her heart swelling with gratitude and sorrow. "Your courage showed me the way. I'll finish what we began."

Guests gathered silently behind her, hearts united in fragile yet determined support. Olivia squared her shoulders, readying herself emotionally and physically for the irreversible final strike.

The mansion's foundations cracked ominously, reality unraveling around them. The Host, utterly vulnerable, struggled weakly against the inevitable, his once-immense power reduced to pathetic whimpers.

Olivia raised her hand decisively, feeling the combined strength of every freed soul, of Julian's sacrifice, and of her own hard-won courage surging through her veins. Her voice, strong and unyielding, echoed powerfully through the collapsing chamber:

"This is your end."

With unstoppable resolve, she prepared to deliver the final, devastating blow, fully aware this moment would define not only her life but countless others—ending centuries of darkness, fear, and despair.

Unmasking Evil

The Host's desperate shriek echoed through the chamber, a final cry filled with fury and fear. Olivia stood firm, heart pounding wildly in her chest as the monstrous form before her twisted and convulsed, shifting grotesquely between corrupted man and primordial horror. His power was unraveling rapidly, but he lunged forward once more, shadows trailing behind him like a living nightmare.

"You will not take this from me!" he roared, voice distorted with rage and panic. Dark tendrils lashed violently, whipping around Olivia, trying desperately to break her resolve.

She ducked, narrowly avoiding his attack, her eyes scanning frantically until they settled on the ornate mirror at the chamber's heart. Suddenly, every journal, every ancient rune clicked vividly in her mind—the mirror. It was the vessel of his immortality, the cursed object tethering countless souls, including her sister's, to eternal torment.

Determined, Olivia raced toward it, but the Host sensed her intent immediately, lurching forward with desperate aggression. Just as her fingers brushed the mirror's cold surface, an explosion of agony ripped through her mind.

She staggered backward as the mirror emitted a piercing cry, conjuring a final, agonizing vision. Julian stood before her, face pale and filled with pleading desperation. "Olivia, stop!" he begged, his voice cracking with raw emotion. "If you destroy this mirror, we'll all be lost forever. You'll doom us to eternal darkness."

For one brief, agonizing moment, Olivia hesitated, her heart torn apart by Julian's voice, his pain unbearably real. Yet, as she stared into his pleading eyes, she saw a subtle emptiness, a hollow shadow beneath his expression. It was a perfect illusion, twisted cruelly by the mirror's desperation to preserve itself.

"No," she whispered defiantly, tears streaming freely down her cheeks. "Julian gave himself freely to end this. He would never beg me to stop. Your lies won't break me again."

With that final declaration, the illusion shattered, dissolving like smoke. Before Olivia could strike, the Host's monstrous form crashed into her, claws gripping her shoulders painfully. They struggled violently, locked in a furious battle amidst the chamber's splintering chaos.

Yet even as pain coursed through her body, Olivia confronted him defiantly, eyes blazing with unyielding courage. "Your immortality is nothing but endless fear. I refuse to let your darkness rule another second!"

His grip faltered momentarily, stunned by her unwavering defiance. Seizing this brief opening, Olivia reached desperately, fingers curling around a fallen piece of broken iron from a nearby candelabra. Summoning all remaining strength, she drove the iron fiercely into the mirror's surface.

The world seemed to pause, a heartbeat of eerie silence before the mirror erupted violently. Shards exploded outward in a dazzling rain of crystal and light, tearing through the Host's monstrous form, ripping him apart with each fragment. Screams of agony filled the chamber as thousands of luminous souls burst forth, rising upward in radiant waves, their gentle whispers of gratitude caressing Olivia like soft, fleeting embraces.

Among the shimmering souls, Olivia saw clearly the serene face of her sister, smiling gently at her, eyes filled with eternal gratitude and peace. Her sister reached out briefly, fingers brushing Olivia's cheek tenderly before fading slowly, finally free from centuries of torment.

"No!" the Host wailed desperately, form disintegrating into shadowy fragments as his immortality fractured. His voice trailed away, reduced to echoes of despair until finally dissolving into silence. His dark legacy, built upon cruelty and fear, unraveled completely, leaving behind only emptiness.

But with the mirror's destruction, the mansion itself began violently collapsing, foundations cracking, walls splitting open as flames erupted spontaneously, devouring remnants of dark enchantments. The floor beneath Olivia's feet shuddered dangerously; reality itself seemed to fracture as the supernatural essence that had bound the mansion for centuries vanished utterly.

Heart racing wildly, Olivia knew she had mere moments to escape. Gathering every ounce of remaining strength, she sprinted frantically toward the chamber's exit, dodging collapsing debris, walls crumbling around her like rotten timber. Fire roared, chasing her through twisting corridors, each passageway collapsing moments after she passed.

Ahead, she glimpsed the surviving guests—Samuel, Lady Evelyn, and Catherine—fleeing desperately, their pale faces reflecting pure terror. Olivia surged forward, adrenaline coursing through her veins, driven by sheer determination to honor Julian's sacrifice and ensure her survival.

Yet, as she neared the mansion's entrance, debris fell violently, blocking her path completely. Olivia halted sharply, panic clawing at her chest as smoke and flames closed in rapidly. She stared desperately at the wreckage, feeling exhaustion claw at her bones.

But as hope flickered dimly, she felt a sudden, comforting presence behind her. Turning briefly, she glimpsed Julian's gentle apparition, his eyes filled with warmth and encouragement. "You're stronger than this, Olivia," he whispered softly. "Live—for both of us."

Empowered by his words, Olivia's determination reignited fiercely. With a desperate cry, she pushed against the wreckage, muscles screaming in agony. Finally, the debris shifted slightly—enough for her to squeeze painfully through, stumbling into the cool, predawn air just as the mansion collapsed spectacularly behind her, erupting into a roaring inferno.

Olivia collapsed onto the damp grass, gasping desperately, feeling the first golden rays of sunrise gently caressing her face. She rolled over, gazing numbly at the mansion's smoldering remains as dawn's gentle light washed away the lingering supernatural darkness. Silence settled softly, broken only by distant crackling flames.

Slowly, Olivia rose, the quiet serenity of morning enveloping her gently. Tears slipped silently down her face as she remembered Julian's courage, her sister's forgiving smile, and the countless souls finally freed. Grief mixed tenderly with profound relief, pain softened by pride and gratitude.

Standing resolutely, she whispered a heartfelt farewell to those she'd lost. "Your courage gave me strength. I promise your sacrifice will never be forgotten."

She walked slowly away from the ruins, leaving behind the smoldering remnants of evil and darkness, each step feeling lighter, freer. Sunlight poured warmly over her shoulders, a new dawn banishing forever the horrors of the Midnight Masquerade.

Olivia stepped forward into the brightening day, determined to live fully, to honor the memories of those she'd loved and lost. As the final shadows faded, she embraced her newfound strength, forever transformed by courage, sacrifice, and redemption—ready to reclaim her life, free at last from the masks that had hidden too many truths for far too long.

Epilogue: Whispers at Dawn

Olivia stood at the edge of the charred grounds, wrapped in the misty embrace of dawn, watching silently as the smoldering ruins of the once-grand manor collapsed slowly into dust. Ethereal flames—silver-white and eerily silent—flickered gently, consuming the last remnants of ancient evil. The sun's pale rays broke through heavy clouds, spreading softly over ashes and stone, chasing away lingering shadows as if to cleanse the ground of its cursed history.

She shivered lightly, exhaustion clinging to her bones, yet feeling a profound calm she'd never known. Julian's sacrifice weighed heavily on her heart, and memories of her sister's gentle farewell remained vivid, both painful and comforting. Their faces lingered in her mind, fragile reminders of love, loss, and courage.

In the weeks that followed, Olivia mourned deeply, quietly visiting Julian's modest memorial near the blackened ruins. Each visit felt heavier, yet oddly healing. She placed fresh flowers gently upon the stone, her whispered promises carried softly by the breeze. "Your courage will never be forgotten," she vowed tenderly. "I'll make sure the world knows your story—even if they don't fully understand."

Life gradually returned, though it felt oddly distant, touched by subtle melancholy and deepened resolve. Friends and colleagues noticed a quiet change in her, sensing layers of pain and strength beneath her reserved smile. Olivia chose carefully, keeping the truth hidden, understanding clearly that the horrors she'd witnessed were beyond belief.

Yet silence was impossible. Olivia felt compelled, duty-bound by those she'd lost, to warn others indirectly. Weeks turned into months as she meticulously crafted her story—an exposé disguised carefully as fiction. Her novel, rich with vivid detail and emotional authenticity, emerged as a chilling yet beautiful tale: a supernatural thriller of hidden societies, haunting mirrors, and souls imprisoned by temptation.

Upon release, the book captivated readers, praised widely for its eerie realism and unsettling emotional depth. The subtle warnings woven within its pages resonated powerfully, though audiences remained unaware of the genuine darkness hidden beneath her fictional veil. Olivia, in quiet interviews, urged readers gently to remain cautious of seductive promises, warning indirectly that beneath masks of elegance lay dangers rooted in human desire.

Yet even as the success of her story brought comfort and closure, Olivia felt a lingering unease—a faint whisper of uncertainty. Dreams troubled her sleep—ghostly echoes of the manor, Julian's voice whispering softly, her sister's gentle smile always just beyond reach. Some nights, she awoke abruptly, heart racing, certain she'd heard faint laughter drifting softly through her window.

Months passed quietly, and the ruins became gently reclaimed by nature. But Olivia sensed something deeper, intangible yet unshakable—a subtle shadow hiding beneath sunlight, waiting patiently for darkness to return. Standing quietly at the edge of the grounds one chilly autumn morning, she heard a soft rustling nearby. Turning sharply, she found only empty silence, yet felt clearly the presence of something watching, waiting.

Elsewhere, beyond her sight, the shadow moved quietly through crowded city streets, unnoticed. An indistinct figure, elegant and ageless, walked silently, hand delivering ornate invitations sealed with crimson wax. Gentle whispers drifted through the air, carried softly by an autumn breeze: *"Come, reveal your truth... if you dare."*

Olivia realized, heart tightening painfully, that the masquerade was eternal—a dance woven from human weakness and desire, destined to repeat endlessly, each generation vulnerable anew. Her victory, while real, had merely delayed inevitable darkness. The Host, diminished yet immortal in essence, awaited patiently, sustained eternally by temptation and fear.

Yet rather than despair, Olivia felt quiet resolve blossom deep within. She would stand ready, vigilant, committed fully to exposing hidden truths, protecting others through words and warnings. Accepting that darkness may never vanish completely, she embraced a life devoted to courage, awareness, and resilience—the only true defenses humanity possessed.

A gentle breeze touched her face softly, carrying faint laughter and whispers, achingly familiar: *"The masquerade awaits. Reveal your truth... if you dare."*

Olivia raised her head defiantly, eyes fierce yet calm, staring resolutely toward the horizon. Yes, the whispers might return forever, the invitations eternal—but so would the courage to resist, to reveal truth, and to stand firm against darkness.

As dawn's soft light warmed her skin, Olivia turned slowly away from the ruins, stepping confidently into the morning. Her quiet voice echoed softly, a promise whispered to the wind:

"I dare."

Bonus Appendix: The Codex of Shadows - Recovered Fragments from the Black Veil Manor

(Compiled from the journals of the lost and the whispers of the damned)

What follows was reconstructed from the remnants I recovered—scorched journals, fractured mirrors, and fragmented whispers left behind in the ashes. Read carefully. Not all truth is safe to know.

THE RUNES AND RULES

"He who enters masked must not remove it. He who seeks truth must first reveal his own."

The Seven Runes of Binding

These symbols were etched into the ritual chamber and the manor's architecture. Translations are speculative.

- *Rúna Noctis* — Mark of eternal twilight. Used to anchor spirits to the mirror realm.
- *Sigil of the Host* — A stylized mask and eye. Represents dominion through deception.
- *The Mirror Veil* — Symbol for illusion, reflection, and imprisonment.
- *Circle of Invitation* — Carved into the ballroom floor. Guests must enter willingly.
- *Rune of Silence* — Prevents victims from crying out truthfully during the masquerade.
- *Sigil of Severance* — Rare. Said to break soul-binding when blood is offered freely.

Bonus Appendix: The Codex of Shadows - Recovered Fragments from t...

> *"It has always been Halloween.*
> *The calendar just forgot."*

Year	Event	Notes
1811	First known masqueerade	Host unnamed in records
1849	Thirteen guests vanished. noo survivors	Reopeened by "Philosophical Society of Inner Desire"
1896	Fire damages west wing	The Host sighted in newspaperphoto
1925	Fire damages west wing	One journal found, then vanished again
1953	Seven disappearances	All footage mysteriously corrupted
2071	Deseps sivors- during invita- tion-only gala	The final masquerade?
20XX	The final masquearade?	Journal fragments recovered post-fire

THE SPECTER OF BLACK VEIL MANOR

Published October 31, 1953 – THE HOLLOW HAVEN LEDGER

"Authorities report no sign of foul play after multiple attendees failed to return from the annual Black Veil gala. Host identified only as "A. Morrow." Guests reportedly left personal belongings behind, including handwritten notes that have since disappeared."

Bonus Chapter: Behind the Scenes

"Every mask hides a face, and behind every face, a story. This one is mine."

The Midnight Masquerade was born at the crossroads of gothic obsession and personal grief. I've always been drawn to haunted mansions, to mirrors that don't just reflect—but *remember*, and to the elegant terror of something too beautiful to trust.

This story grew out of a fascination with **gothic literature**—the atmospheric dread of *Shirley Jackson*, the decaying grandeur of *Poe*, the tragic seduction of *The Picture of Dorian Gray*. I wanted to create a world where temptation wore silk gloves and secrets bled through walls. The idea of a masquerade ball—elegant, opulent, and deeply eerie—felt like the perfect setting to explore the masks we wear and the truths we bury.

But beneath the fiction was something real: **grief**. Like Olivia, I lost someone suddenly and without closure. That wound shaped this book. The supernatural became a lens through which to look at grief, guilt, and memory—how we're haunted, not always by ghosts, but by what we didn't say, by the way someone left us behind.

The **Host** was never just a villain—he was a metaphor for temptation, for every voice that whispers, *"Just one more step... one more lie... one more secret desire fulfilled."* He offered people exactly what they wanted. And in return, he devoured them.

Notes on Character Development

Olivia Grey started as a skeptic. In early drafts, she was more detached, clinical—a journalist chasing a story. But something wasn't working. She needed a reason to *stay* when everything screamed for her to run. That's when her sister's backstory was woven in—and suddenly, Olivia had blood in the game. She wasn't just investigating a mystery; she was hunting a ghost. Her descent into the masquerade became a journey through grief, guilt, and ultimately, redemption.

Julian went through the most transformation. Originally written as a mysterious ally with questionable loyalty, he was meant to die early—a cautionary tale. But the more I wrote him, the more human he became. Broken, brilliant, tormented by choices that weren't entirely his. His story shifted into one of sacrifice. He became the emotional spine of the book—a man trying to undo the damage his desire once wrought. His final act wasn't just heroic—it was an apology.

The Host was always a mask. His real horror wasn't in what he looked like, but what he *offered*: a seductive reflection of your deepest need. I deliberately never gave him a name beyond "A. Morrow" (a play on *a morrow*, or *tomorrow*—he is always just out of reach, promising a better future... for a price).

Catherine, Samuel, and Evelyn were archetypes at first—pride, greed, vanity—but I wanted to blur the lines. Each guest was flawed, yes, but not evil. That's what made their descent more tragic. They weren't chosen because they were wicked, but because they were *ripe*—for temptation, for guilt, for breaking.

Folklore & Mythology Behind the Masquerade

Many threads of folklore are stitched into this story's bones.

• The concept of **mirrors as soul traps** exists in cultures worldwide. In some traditions, mirrors are covered after a death to prevent the soul from being pulled back. That idea twisted beautifully into the mansion's cursed mirrors—objects that *don't just reflect, but devour*.

• The **Faustian bargain**—a deal with a devil in exchange for worldly pleasure—was at the heart of Julian's arc, and more subtly, every guest's. I was particularly influenced by Slavic and Celtic myths where spirits make bargains sealed not with contracts, but with *desire itself*.

• The **manor as a sentient being** owes a nod to haunted house legends—from *Hill House* to *The House of Usher*. But I also drew from the Japanese concept of **tsukumogami**—objects that, after long use or intense emotion, come to life. What if a house *felt* everything that happened inside it... and wanted more?

• The **masquerade** itself is a timeless image. But in Venetian tradition, masks were not only for anonymity—they were believed to blur the line between the physical and spiritual world. That was the seed for the mansion's rule: *"He who enters masked must not remove it."*

Final Reflections

This book isn't just about horror. It's about the choices we make when no one's looking. About what happens when you trade truth for comfort, when you bury pain beneath beauty.

The masquerade is eternal—not just in fiction, but in life. We all wear masks. We all long for something we maybe shouldn't. But in the end, what matters is what we choose to face—and what we choose to let go.

Thank you for stepping into the manor with me. If you ever receive a letter sealed in crimson wax... burn it.

Rowan Hale

Author, Witness, Survivor.

Thematic Discussion Questions
For Book Clubs & Late-Night Fireside Debates

Temptation, Desire & Choice

1 What would you do if your deepest desire could be granted—for a price?

– Where is the line between ambition and obsession?

– Would you have accepted the Host's offer?

2 Is temptation truly evil—or is it only dangerous when acted upon?

– Could the masquerade have been survived without making any deals?

3 Do the guests deserve punishment, or were they victims of manipulation?

– Did they come willingly, or were they lured?

Identity, Masks & Self-Deception

4 Who was the real villain: the Host, or the guests who stayed?

– Did the Host exploit darkness, or merely reveal it?

5 What is Olivia's true "mask," and when does she remove it?

Thematic Discussion Questions

– Does she ever fully take it off, even in the end?

6 Which character's hidden truth shocked you the most?

– What does that reveal about how we judge others?

7 How do masks—literal and symbolic—shape the characters' actions and identities?

– What are the dangers of hiding behind a persona?

Grief, Memory & Redemption

8 Was Julian redeemed in the end?

– Does a selfless act atone for past sins, even horrific ones?

9 What role does grief play in the story?

– Is Olivia trying to rescue her sister—or forgive herself?

10 Do you believe the mansion was truly evil… or just a mirror of those who entered it?

– Could it have been a test, not a trap?

Myth, Madness & the Supernatural

11 Did the supernatural elements feel like metaphors for psychological truths?

– Could the entire masquerade be seen as a descent into Olivia's subconscious?

12 The Host is defeated, but the masquerade survives. What does that say about evil—can it be destroyed, or only delayed?

– Is the cycle inevitable?

Bonus: For Creative Readers

13 If you were invited to the next masquerade, what would your mask look like—and what truth would it hide?

14 Write a final letter from Olivia to Julian. What would she say that she never got to?

www.ingramcontent.com/pod-product-compliance
Lightning Source LLC
LaVergne TN
LVHW050025080526
838202LV00069B/6921